# Pigs Can Fly!

# Pigs Can Fly!

## The Adventures of Harriet Pig and Friends

## Debbi Chocolate

### Illustrated by Leslie Tryon

Library of Congress Cataloging-in-Publication Data

Chocolate, Deborah M. Newton.
  Pigs can fly! : the adventures of Harriet Pig and friends / Debbi Chocolate ; illustrated by Leslie Tryon.— 1st American ed.
      p. cm.
Summary: In four stories, Harriet Pig realizes her dream to fly, helps a friend overcome a fear of heights, trains for a swim race against a boastful goose, and more than repays the mouse who saved her life.
  ISBN 0-8126-2706-7 (cloth : alk. paper)
  [1. Pigs—Fiction. 2. Animals—Fiction.] I. Tryon, Leslie, ill. II. Title.
  PZ7.C44624Pk 2004
  [E]—dc22
                                                              2003016504

For Jane Jordan Browne, mentor and friend.
    —D.C.

In memory of Harriet, who taught me how to dance.
    —L.T.

# Contents

# Pigs Can Fly!

# Pigs Can Fly!

Once upon a time there was a potbellied pig named Harriet. More than anything in the world, Harriet wanted to fly. She loved her red cape. Whenever she wore it, she felt like anything was possible—especially flying.

Harriet and her cape were inseparable.

She wore it to school.

She wore it to ballet lessons.

She even wore it to bed at night.

Sometimes Harriet imagined she was Super Pig, able to leap tall buildings in a single bound.

1

Sometimes she imagined she was Eagle Pig, able to soar to new and fantastic heights.

And sometimes Harriet imagined she was a World War I flying ace, going on secret missions in the dark blue night.

Deep down in her heart, Harriet knew that one day she would fly. So she was always ready for the moment when she would make it happen.

"Pigs can't fly!" snorted Harriet's Aunt Mabel.
"Quite right!" said Harriet's stuffy Uncle
Winkle. "Why, if pigs could fly, they'd have
wings."

3

Harriet would not listen to Aunt Mabel. She would not listen to Uncle Winkle. Harriet wanted to fly.

So she tried parachuting.

But the parachute didn't pop.

She tried bungee jumping.

But the bungee cord didn't jump.

She tried hot air ballooning.

But all the hot air fizzled out.

She even tried flying like an acrobat.

But instead, she ended up hanging onto the trapeze bar by one hoof, upside down!

Then one day at school the teacher announced, "Now, children, there are lots of parts, but who wants to be the *fairy* in this year's spring play?" Harriet trembled with delight. This was the moment she had been waiting for. She knew fairies could fly. So she raised one pink hoof.

At the desk beside her, a squeaky little voice said, "Pigs can't fly!" It was Homer, the gray mouse. He hadn't raised his paw.

Harriet's cheeks turned bright red. But she kept her dainty pink hoof up in the air anyway.

"Tryouts on Monday," said Ms. Glad.

At Saturday ballet class, Harriet wiggled into her tutu.

She spent all of Saturday afternoon learning to leap like a fairy.

She spent all of Sunday soaking her sore little pink hooves.

Monday morning, Harriet sat at her desk holding her breath. When it was her turn to audition, Harriet leaped and danced down the aisles, almost like a real fairy. She was magnificent.

Homer didn't think Harriet was magnificent. The sight of a leaping pig made him tremble with fear. Homer was so frightened he ran to a corner and hid. But there was no escaping Harriet's big leaping shadow.

Later that day, Harriet couldn't believe her ears when Ms. Glad announced to the class, "Harriet will be our fairy this spring."

On the big night, Harriet squeezed into her costume. From backstage she heard the music start. She peeked through the curtain. The house lights dimmed. The stage lights brightened. And then the play began. In the glow of the spotlight Harriet found herself flying high out

over the audience, sprinkling shimmering fairy
dust. Her costume was rigged to stage wires
that reached from the tall ceiling of the assembly
hall all the way down to the adoring crowd.
Harriet was actually flying. It was just like she
had always imagined it.

. . . Leaping in a single bound,

. . . soaring to fantastic heights,

. . . and flying in the deep dark night.

By the time the curtain fell—a star had been born!

Amidst the roaring of the curtain call, the crowd began to chant: "*Har-ri-et! Har-ri-et! Har-ri-et!*" Standing in the spotlight at center

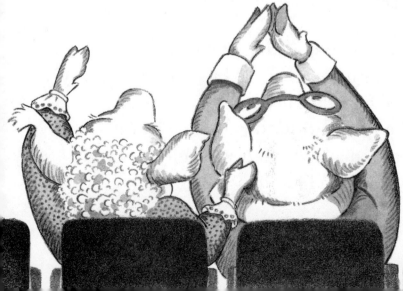

stage, Harriet peered out into the audience and saw two familiar faces.

"Aunt Mabel! Uncle Winkle!" shouted Harriet, waving wildly.

Sitting in the row next to Aunt Mabel and Uncle Winkle was Homer Mouse. Homer, covered in shimmering fairy dust, was in a state of shock. He was still trembling from the scary thought that during her performance Harriet's wires could have snapped, sending her crashing down onto the front-row seat where he sat.

Suddenly Aunt Mabel and Uncle Winkle leaped from their seats. They helped Harriet weave her way from the stage through the cheering applause.

Once outside, Uncle Winkle flagged down a taxicab.

"Harriet!" squealed Aunt Mabel at breakfast the next morning. "You made the news!" Aunt Mabel was so excited she could hardly sit still.

"Yes, indeed you did!" snorted Uncle Winkle, handing Harriet a copy of *The Evening Post*.

Starry-eyed, Harriet took the paper from Uncle Winkle. On the front page was a big picture of her sprinkling fairy dust from high out over the audience on a tiny gray mouse in a front-row seat. It was Homer!

In the picture, Harriet's fairy costume fit snug as a bug. Above the picture, in big bold print, was the headline: *Pigs Can Fly!*

"Yes they can!" said Harriet happily. "They certainly *can!*"

# By the Silvery Moon

Penny Porcupine was afraid of heights.

She didn't climb trees like other porcupines, so she didn't nap in trees like other porcupines.

And she was always polishing her claws with fingernail polish.

It was no surprise that the other porcupines thought Penny was just a *little* strange.

One day, Harriet Pig invited Penny on a roller-coaster ride.

"It's the world's tallest roller coaster!" squealed Harriet. She showed Penny a picture of the roller coaster in the entertainment section of *The Evening Post*. Just looking at the picture made Penny's quills stand up. Penny was too embarrassed to tell Harriet she was afraid of heights, so she didn't say anything.

That afternoon at the amusement park, the roller-coaster cars clicked their way high up over a curved track, then stopped in midair. Penny took a deep breath. Suddenly, without warning and with blinding speed, the roller coaster raced down the steep track toward the amusement stands. Harriet screamed and squealed with delight and waved her little pink hooves in the air. Penny held on for dear life. By the time the roller coaster came to a standstill, Penny's knuckles had turned white.

"You're afraid of heights?" exclaimed Harriet. "We'll have to fix that!"

Right away, Penny could see that Harriet meant business. In her little porcupine mind, Penny imagined herself the first porcupine ever launched from Harriet's colossal, silver catapult—*Boi-yoing!*

*Adios!*

*Sayonara!*

*See yuh!*

*Good-bye!*

In her prickly little head, Penny imagined being bolted clear across the world, way over the Great Wall of China. *Ouch! That hurt!*

<u>Rest in Peace, Penny!</u>

  2 short
+<u>2 be</u>
  4 gotten

These wild imaginings left Penny feeling frightened. Yet wild imaginings were all they were. For Harriet didn't own a colossal, silver catapult. She certainly didn't own anything that could bolt Penny way over the Great Wall of China.

But what Harriet did own was a flaming red silk scarf that she flung dramatically around Penny's neck. And a World War I pilot suit and goggles, which she dressed Penny in. Then Harriet helped Penny climb into the cockpit of her own hand-built SS *Flying Tiger*.

Harriet turned on an electric fan that clamored and sputtered like an old airplane engine. The blast from the fan nearly blew Penny out of the cockpit. *This is it!* quivered Penny, now nearly in tears.

Penny's quills flinched. Harriet shouted over the noise of the sputtering fan: "Not to worry! This is only a ground test!"

Penny nodded. Then the two friends gave each other a thumbs up.

Harriet backed away from the *Flying Tiger*. "All engines go!" she yelled.

With her red silk scarf flying in the wind, Penny pretended to rev the engine. "Prepare for takeoff!" Harriet shouted.

As Penny hunkered down in the pilot's seat, half crazy with fear, half crazy with excitement, Harriet waved her flags and shouted, *"Let her rip!"*

Although Penny never really left the ground, the sputtering engine and whipping wind made her feel as though she were gliding on air, way up in the clouds.

Meanwhile, through the thick fog, Penny imagined that she could see Harriet down on the ground—waving flags and flashlights, directing her heroic flight.

In a flurry of parade confetti, Penny made a dramatic descent. No longer Penny the fearful porcupine, Penny was now a World War I flying ace!

Next came a test with even higher stakes. Harriet tried coaxing the stout porcupine onto a kitchen chair.

"Come on," pleaded Harriet. "It's the next step."

But Penny, who was busy polishing her toenails, flashed her freshly painted pink claws at Harriet.

"I can't," she said. "My nails are wet.

We'll have to wait, I guess." Little did Penny know—Harriet had no idea what the word "wait" meant.

Harriet flung open the kitchen door where outside a mariachi band playing salsa, merengue, and samba music was in full swing. Penny tried to sit still. But before she knew it, she was dancing to the beat of a catchy samba tune.

It didn't take long before Penny *really* cut loose. Caught up in the moment, Penny snatched a long-stemmed daisy from the window vase. She clenched the flower between her teeth and strutted like a bullfighting matador, or like a swaggering flamenco dancer. Then she danced all over the kitchen, shouting, "*Olé!*" to anyone who would listen.

Seeing her opportunity, Harriet coaxed the dancing Penny onto a chair. Finally, she coaxed Penny onto the kitchen table. Before it was over, Penny refused to come down unless Harriet would promise to teach her to dance the cha-cha and the tango.

Penny did not know that even *higher* stakes
were just around the corner.

"*Bombs awaaaaay!*" yelled Harriet at the top of her lungs as she jumped from the "yikes-too-tall" diving board into the swimming pool below. Dressed in a hot pink bikini, Penny stood trembling at the back of the diving board. Staring down into the water, which seemed miles and miles away, Penny flinched when Harriet suddenly surfaced from the water and yelled: "Now that's what you call a perfect cannonball! Now *you* try it! Just jump, curl, and splash."

"Okay," said Penny in a weak voice. But even as she spoke, Penny's freshly polished toenails scratched deep into the surface of the diving board. With her heart pounding in her ears, Penny tried to leap, but her nails refused to let go. Harriet watched with curiosity as Penny hung upside down by her toes, blowing like a sheet in the wind.

"Okay. All right," said Harriet, climbing up to the diving board. Harriet loosened Penny's claws one by one and stood her upright.

Harriet tried squeezing Penny into a pink plastic life preserver. "This," she explained "will help soften your jump." But as Harriet wrestled the life preserver over Penny's head, Penny's quills stood straight up and punctured the life out of the life preserver. And like the life preserver, Penny looked deflated, too.

"Not to worry," said Harriet, looking doubtfully at her friend. "There's still hope." Harriet didn't look like she believed a word she'd said.

As lunch hour approached, Harriet got an idea. She threw a block of salt into the pool. Salt was Penny's favorite food. Penny waddled to the edge of the diving board. As she stared down at the salt block, her mouth began

to water and spout like a water slide at an amusement park. Penny lay down on her belly and clawed at the air.

Harriet shouted up at her, "It's jump, curl, splash! Jump, curl, splash!" But Penny didn't jump, curl, or splash. She was too scared to do that. Penny gave Harriet a weak smile and nod.

Harriet had seen enough. Once again, she climbed the ladder up to the diving board.

Together the two friends stood on the edge of the board. All of a sudden, Harriet leaped off the board, taking Penny with her. It was *jump, curl, splash!* right into the water.

"*Whoa!*" yelled Penny. "That was *cold!*" And then she

admitted weakly, "And fun, too."

Penny waddled up the ladder to the diving board, this time *all alone.* When she reached the top, she waddled to the diving board's edge and dove into the water—*jump, curl, splash!* All by herself.

For the remainder of the day all Penny did was *jump, curl, splash! Jump, curl, splash!* (In between jumps, Penny couldn't resist licking the salt block sitting in the middle of the pool.) And by late afternoon, Penny's cannonballs were even more perfect than Harriet's.

At bedtime, Harriet saw a dark figure bouncing off the diving board. It was Penny. She was *still* diving, by the light of the moon. That was why at sunrise the next morning, Harriet was surprised to see Penny standing at her door.

Decked out in mountain-climbing gear, with ropes, grips, and boots, Penny threw her head back and announced in a confident voice,

"Rise and shine, Harriet! Yesterday, the world's tallest roller coaster! Today, the Himalaya Mountains!" And then she winked at Harriet and said, "It's the next step, my friend."

# Waikiki or Bust!

Lucy Goosey swam like a champ.

And boy was she fast!

She swam the front stroke like lightning.

She swam the backstroke as strong as thunder.

And she was absolutely stunning when it came to the sidestroke. Lucy Goosey swam the sidestroke so fast you couldn't even *see* her when she swam past.

Lucy Goosey certainly was a champ when it came to swimming. But she was more than that.

When it came to swimming, Lucy Goosey was the fastest goose in the whole wide gaggle.

One day, Lucy Goosey challenged Harriet Pig and Hillary Hippopotamus to a swimming contest.

"Just a friendly competition. To see who's best," said snooty Lucy.

"*Harriet!*" whispered Hillary Hippopotamus. "Don't fall for it. Lucy knows we can't beat her. She's just showing off."

"It's a bet!" said Harriet, beaming with confidence.

Harriet and Hillary wasted no time. That very day, the two friends went to the pool to practice their swim stroke.

But not Lucy Goosey. Why should she? As a goose and a champion swimmer, Lucy was more than likely to win the contest without even trying. While Harriet and Hillary were busy practicing and getting into shape, Lucy busied herself with her favorite pastime: baking pies, strawberry tortes, triple-layered double-chocolate fudge cakes, and crumbly thumb-print butter cookies.

Waiting for her pastries to bake, Lucy licked clean her baking spoon. Licking the baking spoon led Lucy to licking the mixing bowl. And then, not surprisingly, as soon as her first tray of pastries was done, Lucy began nibbling on her sweet confections.

While Harriet and Hillary practiced and trained, Lucy spent the next three days nibbling

away on sweets, until finally her webbed feet all but disappeared right from under her. (Lucy's feet hadn't really disappeared. They were hiding beneath her belly.)

The next afternoon, Lucy waddled over to the pool with her freshly baked goodies. There she found Harriet and Hillary working hard preparing for the race.

"Who will help me eat my sweets?" she sang cheerily.

"Not I," answered Harriet, her little pink snout twitching and trembling at the sweet aroma of triple-layered double-chocolate fudge cake, strawberry tortes, blueberry pie, and thumb-print butter cookies. "For I," Harriet forced herself to say, "am doing chin-ups in preparation for the big race."

Now Harriet loved sweets. And it was true, she was trying to keep her chin up, all right. But what was really on her mind was how she would just love to sink her teeth into Lucy's deep,

dark, triple-layered double-chocolate fudge
cake. All the while that Harriet talked to Lucy,
she kept a calm, straight face. But underneath
her calm, Harriet could definitely feel a case of
the screaming-chocolate-me-me's coming on.

Next, Lucy Goosey turned to Hillary with
her oven-baked treats.

"Who will help me eat my sweets?" sang Lucy cheerily.

"Not I," answered Hillary, perspiring profusely. The smell of thumb-print butter cookies made Hillary's nose swell to twice its normal size. For though Lucy didn't know it, butter cookies just happened to be Hillary's secret weakness. "For I," continued Hillary, choking back fat hippo tears, "am busy doing push-ups, preparing for the big race."

"Well!" snipped snooty Lucy, "then the more and the merrier for me!"

Meanwhile, with each passing day of baking, Lucy Goosey's belly was getting
bigger
. . . and bigger
. . . and bigger!
Now instead of practicing for the big race, Lucy spent the remaining days floating belly up in the pool, hiding behind an outrageous pair of designer sunglasses. (She was secretly trying to keep tabs on the competition.)

31

Out of politeness, Hillary pretended not to recognize her archrival. But as soon as Lucy floated by, Hillary whispered to Harriet, "Psssssst! Hey! Isn't that Lucy Goosey?"

"How can you tell?" asked Harriet, eyeing the white butterball-of-a-thing floating by on wings.

"By the sunglasses," giggled Hillary.

Needless to say, by the day of the swimming contest, Lucy was as fat as an Easter egg. But that didn't stop her from squeezing into a tiny, two-piece bikini and cannonballing into the pool for a sneaky head start.

"*Waikiki or bust!*" shouted Lucy as she plunged into the pool and drifted belly up. "The winner will be the first to finish three whole lengths! *Bon voyage!*" She yelled and splashed—paddling furiously but getting nowhere fast.

Harriet and Hillary plunged into the pool, too, and the race began!

Harriet and Hillary quickly swam past Lucy and outdistanced her by half a length. But Lucy, the

champion swimmer that she was, soon found her stride. And with only two lengths left, Lucy pulled up at their side. Now all three were neck and neck—and neck.

Gliding underwater, Hillary surged ahead. Harriet, stroking furiously, switched to her breaststroke and took the lead. The race was in full heat when a sudden reversal of fortune hit. Lucy Goosey switched to her stunning sidestroke and lit past the two friends at a blinding speed. Streaking like a bolt of lightning, Lucy was beating her rivals with only one length left.

It was Lucy ahead at the half length! Lucy ahead at the quarter length! Lucy stroking the water as she had never stroked before! (While inside Lucy's belly a breakfast of sugary-sweet confections was growling and churning with a tiny roar.)

Suddenly, her belly bloated from a breakfast of blueberry pie, Lucy Goosey ducked underneath the water.

Less than an arm's length behind and swimming neck and neck, Harriet and Hillary raced toward the finish. Harriet leaped like a trout, winning the race by her little pink snout. The two friends splashed and hugged. Then Hillary proclaimed, "Meet Harriet, the new champ!"

Later, while Harriet and Hillary feasted on Lucy's triple-layered double-chocolate fudge cake, while they savored Lucy's tortes and thumbprint cookies, Lucy busied herself by packing her suitcase for warmer waters.

"Well," said Lucy, "it's been awful sweet. But summer's over. Time to fly south. *Waikiki! Waikiki*, here I come or *bust!*"

Lucy was decked out in an extra-large designer muumuu gown and a designer floradora beach hat. The floradora's flashy display of colorful straw flowers bounced with Lucy's every waddling step.

On her feet, which she still couldn't see, Lucy wore Birkenstock sandals. And it goes without saying that she was indeed wearing her *totally*

outrageous designer sunglasses. No, Lucy wasn't a champion swimmer anymore. Now she was more like a superstar!

Munching on thumb-print butter cookies, Hillary did a double take on Lucy's extra-large, designer muumuu outfit.

Ever so delicately and gently, Hillary raised the million-dollar question: "Lucy," she said, "just how *are* you going to fly?"

Without hesitating, Lucy waved an airplane ticket in the air. "First class!" laughed Lucy Goosey. "*First class!*"

# Just Friends

Homer Mouse was a seafaring young chap.

He loved his little boat.

He loved the feel of wind in his hair and the smell of sea salt in his tiny, little mouse nose.

But most of all, Homer loved being alone.

Yes, Homer was an old salt, all right. But he was more than that.

In a manner of speaking, Homer was his own man. For he was, beyond all else, the captain of his own boat.

One morning, as Homer prepared to launch his boat, he heard a shrill cry: "*Helllp! Save me!*" The voice sounded awfully familiar. But Homer couldn't be sure. To Homer, the cry sounded like it was coming from a pig staring into a breakfast plate of ham and eggs.

"*Helllp! Please!*"

At the stern of the boat, to his surprise, Homer saw two little pink hooves waving frantically from the water. Then he saw a flaming red cape. A pink snout. And immediately, Homer knew to whom the voice belonged.

"*Helllp!*" Homer wasted no time in throwing out a line. He lowered his motorized crane. Then, with his big, big engine he slowly and carefully lifted the flaming red cape (with the little pink hooves and snout attached) slowly out of the water.

In her drenched cape, Harriet looked like a very wet superhero. No sooner had Harriet landed on deck than she began kissing and hugging the very life out of tiny, little Homer.

"Oh, Homer!" squealed Harriet. "Homer, Homer, Homer!" she went on and on. "Homer! You saved my life! I couldn't swim. My hooves were tangled in my cape. How will I ever repay you?"

Homer looked at Harriet out of the corner of his eye. Under his breath he replied, "Well, you might begin by getting off my boat!" But Harriet didn't hear Homer's whisperings. She kept right on hugging and kissing and squeezing the life out of her new best friend.

The next morning, Homer awoke to the delicious smell of cheddar cheese omelets. The sound of clanging buckets above deck told Homer someone was mopping and sloshing down his deck. When he climbed up top, Homer discovered Harriet dressed in a mid-shipman's uniform, mopping and singing a hearty "Anchors Away!"

As soon as she saw Homer she saluted him

and shouted, "Aye, aye, captain! Breakfast is served! The deck is shipshape! All present and accounted for, sir!"

Homer covered his tiny, little mouse ears. "Harriet," he pleaded, "what are you doing aboard my boat?"

"Sir, you saved my life, sir!" shouted Harriet. "I'm trying to repay you, sir!"

"Harriet!" squealed Homer. "Please stop shouting!"

"Sir, yes, sir," said Harriet more calmly.

"Listen," said Homer, trying to appeal to Harriet's common sense, "you don't owe me anything. I would have done the same for any of my friends."

"Sir, yes, sir," said Harriet, smiling softly. And then she pounced upon the pint-sized mouse with a great, big old bear hug and squeeze.

Later that afternoon Harriet returned. She brought along a giant, steaming hot, cheese burrito. Now it was a fact that Homer loved cheese. After all *he was a mouse*! Much to his dismay, Homer just couldn't resist the giant cheese burrito. Homer ate burrito until his cheeks turned green. He got very sick. He wished that Harriet would just go away. But she didn't.

The next day, Harriet gave Homer a cape as flaming red as her own.

"My hero!" exclaimed Harriet as they looked in the mirror. But the cape wasn't a very good fit. Everywhere Homer went, the flaming red hem kept tripping up his feet. The whole town was laughing at Homer's expense.

Next, Harriet had Homer fitted for a tuxedo. When Homer was finally dressed in the tiniest tuxedo anybody ever saw, Harriet dragged him off to the annual Animals' Ball. She thought she was doing him a big favor. All the other animals were cutting up and having a ball, but not Homer. There was nobody Homer's size to dance with. So Harriet danced every dance with Homer. She flung him into the air and pounced on him all night long.

That evening, Homer decided he'd had enough. He lay awake in his bunk all night trying to think of a way to stop Harriet from feeling she owed him for saving his life. It wasn't long before Homer came up with a few brilliant ideas.

At sunrise, as Harriet sloshed down the deck, Homer asked his friend to paint the deck red when she was done. Harriet didn't mind. Red was Harriet's favorite color.

When she was done painting the deck, Homer next asked Harriet to paint the hull of the boat sky blue. Then he asked her to load, then unload the cargo hold. And when she was finished with that, Homer asked her to grease the big, big engine.

Harriet was becoming a little unraveled. But clearly she wasn't ready to give up yet. So Homer asked Harriet to go to the general store to pick up a little order for him.

"A little order?" asked Harriet. She was breathing quite heavily now from having performed such tiring work.

"Yes! Cheese!" smiled Homer. "I'm making cheesecake," he added, his eyes twinkling a bit.

At the general store, Harriet quickly discovered that Homer's "little order" was a whole *barrel* of cheese. As she made her way home, huffing and puffing, Harriet was so tired she nearly collapsed. But somehow, she managed to get the cheese home to her cottage.

"And now," smiled Homer when he arrived at Harriet's, "will you help me bake my cheesecake, please?"

"Now?!!!" squealed Harriet shrilly. She had just about reached the end of her rope.

"Yes, friend," replied Homer. He was wearing a chef's hat and apron. He handed Harriet a chef's hat and apron, too. "You do the cooking."

"Yes . . . sir," said Harriet weakly. Homer was very pleased with himself. His plan to tire Harriet out was working better than he had expected.

By now dog-tired, in the cozy warmth of the kitchen, Harriet kept nodding in and out of sleep. Homer saw his chance. He climbed up on the kitchen table. He scrambled up the wooden baker's spoon. And then, Homer closed his eyes and jumped with a splash right down into the cheesy batter.

"*Helllp! Save me!*" squealed Homer, thrashing and splashing wildly about. "*Helllp! Please!*"

A startled Harriet flinched wide awake. Where was Homer?

"*Helllp!*" she heard a tiny, squealing voice. "*Helllp! Save me!*" Harriet looked down into the mixing bowl. Something was swimming in the batter. *It was Homer!*

Harriet grabbed the baking spoon and scooped Homer right out.

"Oh, Harriet!" squealed Homer. "Harriet, Harriet, Harriet!" he went on and on. "Harriet! You saved my life! How will I ever repay you?"

"You don't owe me," said Harriet. "I would have done the same for any of my friends."

"Me, too," said Homer licking the cheese off his chin.

"Homer," asked Harriet thoughtfully, "how's about we go back to being just friends again?"

"Just friends?" said Homer.

"Just friends," repeated Harriet. And then she nearly squeezed the cheese out of Homer by giving him a great, big bear hug.